The Adventures of
Officer Zach and K9 Henry

ISBN 978-1-0980-6439-6 (paperback)
ISBN 978-1-0980-6440-2 (hardcover)
ISBN 978-1-0980-6441-9 (digital)

Christian Faith Publishing, Inc.
832 Park Avenue
Meadville, PA 16335
www.christianfaithpublishing.com

Printed in the United States of America

The Adventures of
Officer Zach and K9 Henry

Lisa Faris

Henry loved summer afternoons. Henry was a dog, and he loved to nap on the back porch in the sun while Zach ate his lunch. Zach was Henry's boy, and he had a great imagination and could always find something fun for them to do.

This afternoon was going to be super fun. Zach had gotten a battery-powered truck for his birthday, and he had spent the morning getting it all fixed up for their afternoon. Zach cut out letters that spelled P-O-L-I-C-E and taped them on both sides of the truck. On the back, he taped the letter K and a number 9. This week, Zach wanted to be a police officer, and Henry would be his K9 partner.

Henry heard the back door open and jumped up with his tail wagging. It was time to go to work. Zach had a big gold star on his shirt and his walky-talkies with him.

"Come on, Henry," Zach said, "let's patrol our street."

Henry ran after Zach as they headed to the truck. Zach got in the truck, and Henry jumped in after him. Zach placed one walkie-talkie in the truck and clipped the other on his belt. Then he clipped another gold start to Henry's collar. They were ready to patrol.

The started out of the driveway and headed down the sidewalk toward Mrs. Cooper's house. She worked in her yard every afternoon, and Henry liked Mrs. Cooper. She always had candy and yummy dog treats in her apron pocket.

On their way down the street, they saw Daisy sitting on the curb crying. Daisy was the little girl who lived next door to Zach. Officer Zach stopped his truck and asked, "What's wrong, Daisy?"

Daisy sniffled and said, "Boots is missing, I can't find him anywhere."

Boots was Daisy's new kitty. Henry loved to bark and play chase with Boots.

Zach looked at Henry and said, "This sounds like a job for us, K9 Henry."

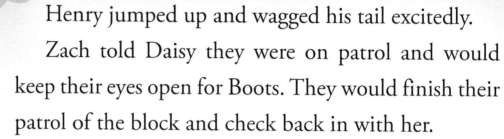

Henry jumped up and wagged his tail excitedly. Zach told Daisy they were on patrol and would keep their eyes open for Boots. They would finish their patrol of the block and check back in with her.

"Thank you, Officer Zach," Daisy said.

Off they went. Henry didn't know where or how to look for Boots, so he rode along quietly while Zach drove them toward Mrs. Cooper's yard.

Mrs. Cooper waved hello and was ready to greet her two favorite police officers with snacks. Henry was wagging his tail when she offered Zach a candy and reached into her pocket for a treat for him.

Zach munched on his candy and told Mrs. Cooper about Daisy and Boots while Henry was quietly sniffing Mrs. Cooper's rose bushes. Wait… Henry heard something!

It sounded like someone was needing help, but where? Henry took off running and stopped at the tree across the yard. It was Boots. Boots was way up in the tree and was meowing like he was really scared. He wondered how Boots even get up there.

Henry started to bark, and that brought Zach and Mrs. Cooper to see what all the fuss was about.

"Well, look at that," Mrs. Cooper said. Henry found Boots.

Mrs. Cooper told Zach to run next door to Mr. Randall's house and ask him to bring his ladder. With Mr. Randall's help, they had Boots down in no time. Mr. Randall told them that cats love to climb trees, but sometimes, they get too high and can't get themselves back down. It was a good thing Henry heard him meowing or he could have been stuck up there a long time.

It was time to get Boots back home to Daisy. Henry jumped back in the truck, and Officer Zach carried Boots while he drove very slowly back to Daisy's house. Boots was still meowing, but he was very glad to be out of the tree.

Daisy was still sitting on the curb and was very happy to see Boots.

Zach told her how Henry heard Boots meowing in the tree and called for backup. Daisy said, "Henry is a hero," and thanked them both for saving her kitty.

Zach and Henry headed home and reported to Mom about their rescue. She was very proud of her two officers and decided that they deserved a special dinner. Henry got excited as Zach jumped up and down singing, "Cheeseburgers, cheeseburgers!"

About the Author

Lisa Faris started creating stories in 2005 to entertain her son when he was little. She decided to start writing about these stories to share them with others, including her grandchildren. She enjoys spending time with her family and their pets and loves to inspire kids to use their imaginations. She lives with her family and dogs in Northern Nevada.

CPSIA information can be obtained
at www.ICGtesting.com
Printed in the USA
BVHW092124301121
622780BV00006B/336

9 781098 064402